About Leaf Books

Our mission is to provide readers with a pocket-sized read in the places where they are waiting, relaxing, taking a break. We aim to support writers by giving them a new market for their short stories and short non-fiction.

Don't forget to visit our website www.leafbooks.co.uk to tell us what you think of this book and to learn more about the writer and our other services.

Enjoy!

First published by Leaf Books Ltd in 2006
Copyright © Maria Donovan

Cover illustration © David Fisher

Leaf Books are proud to be working with
The University of Glamorgan

www.leafbooks.co.uk

Leaf
GTi Suite,
Valleys Innovation Centre,
Navigation Park,
Abercynon,
CF45 4SN

Printed by Allprint
www.allprint.ltd.uk

ISBN 1-905599-16-1
ISBN 978-1905599-16-5

Tea for
Mr Dead

Short short stories

by

Maria Donovan

Maria Donovan

Maria was brought up in Dorset and lived in Holland for many years. She has worked as a nurse, gardener and magician's assistant. In 1997 she came to Wales and enrolled as an undergraduate at the University of Glamorgan in order to make writing the focus of her working life. Now a Lecturer in Creative Writing at Glamorgan, she has recently completed an MPhil in Writing. Longer short stories have appeared in *Mslexia*, *New Welsh Review* and the Honno anthology *My Cheating Heart*. Her first collection of longer stories, *Pumping Up Napoleon*, will be published by Seren in 2007.

Contents

Acknowledgements

'The Longest Date', 'Frog face', 'House Demons', 'Sleep Bank', 'Legs in the Window', 'School Fete' and 'The Butcher's Wife' were originally published by the-phone-book.com

Legs in the Window

A pair of brown furry legs is sticking out of the window of No 73. The window is on the ground floor but the only part that opens is above head height. It looks as if a big cuddly bear got his tummy stuck as he tried to climb back into the playroom. The legs are waggling.

Up on the mountain, students foam out of the Union bars. Soon they'll be surging down this terraced street, singing, pushing the wheely-bins around, shouting, 'I love you.'

Meanwhile a girl in a black jacket comes walking; her heels tap; the bear holds his legs still – as if he is listening. She passes underneath them without looking, unlocks the door and goes inside.

Half a minute later the upstairs light comes on. Slowly, the bear lets his legs droop, but his paws won't reach the ground.

A Student Nurse on Holiday

The pregnant woman hasn't touched her dessert. As the train runs west she leaves the table and lurches east down the aisle. What would happen if she were to go into labour, miles between stations, perhaps in the toilet, perhaps right here in the dining-car?

You would send the waiter for ironed linen and hot water; tell him to telephone ahead. You'd get down on the shaking floor.

What if the baby gets stuck? Which spoons make the best forceps?

The pregnant woman has not come back. Is she jammed in the loo? A train toilet makes an unsuitable birthing stool. Should you go and look? Hammer on the locked door? Pull the communication cord? Speak to the conductor?

You go on eating as if nothing has happened. No one hears the rattle of your heart above the rhythm of the train.

The Last Breakfast

The nurse arrived on duty at 7.30am determined not to make any more silly mistakes. She changed into uniform and, being the first to arrive, started to serve breakfast from the waiting car.

The others arrived when she was halfway down the corridor; they were laughing about something that had happened the night before. At the end of the corridor she carried a bowl of porridge on a tray into Room 121 and was already nearing the bed, towards which several occupied chairs were turned, before she realised that the supine woman they were all looking at was dead and that the many people around her at that early hour were crying and holding hands. Every reddened eye turned towards her as she backed away and tried to hide what she had brought: the tray, the bowl and the spoon.

School Fête

'You've got to be careful with electricity,' says Mavis as they approach the stall. Jack gives a loud snort.

'Silly old thing,' he says.

The man in charge of the game smiles. 'Have a go; it's quite safe. Hi, Mavis.'

'Hi, Frank.'

'You know each other?' says Jack.

'He's a dad,' says Mavis.

'Have a go,' repeats Frank. 'It's quite safe.'

'Yeah,' say Jack. 'It's just a game, see? You've got to pass the loop all along the wiggly wire, round the bends and all that without touching it, cos every time you do, a buzzer goes off. Irritating yes; dangerous, no.' Jack grasps the stick with the wire loop at the end. 'I'll show you how it's done then you can try.' He frowns and begins.

'Nice day,' says Mavis.

'Marvellous,' says Frank.

Jack ought to wonder why his wife isn't champing to get to the cake stall, but he's too busy concentrating on not making a connection.

Break

'It will be all right, won't it, nurse?' he says. We both look down at his wife. Primary cancer, metastases in the bones.

I say to him: 'We'll try to make her comfortable, Mr Jones. We're hoping to get her a special bed soon.'

There are tears in his eyes and mine. I'd like to touch his hand but instead I pat her pillow and pull the collar of her nightie closed. It's not her nightie really, but one of ours, one that's been left behind. It has two buttons missing at the neck. But she's doubly incontinent (type and quantity) and he can't keep up with the washing. It's a small thing we can do, like letting him have a cup of tea when the trolley comes round.

The corridor is empty. The others are on their mid-morning break. I try to make it to the staff room before anyone else can ring their bell. I need coffee.

My colleagues are sitting in a circle around

a low table, chatting, laughing and smoking. A patient has gone home and left a tray of cream cakes in parting thanks. As usual I think about not eating one. As usual I decide that life's too short.

The head nurse, licking cream from her fingers, is telling a story about when she was a student. 'As I took the first of the stitches out the whole wound just burst open; blood everywhere.' She shakes her head. 'I was terrified; thought I'd done something wrong. But you know it was just one of those things. So don't worry…' She pats the arm of the anxious student next to her. 'I'm sure it won't be as bad as that your first time.'

A bell rings. Groans all round. 'I'll go,' I say, putting down my cake and getting up. No one tries to stop me. I'm halfway down the corridor before I feel any resentment. What is it with me? Last to sit down, first to get up? What am I trying to prove?

*

It's Mr Jones. 'Oh dear, nurse,' he says (he can never remember our names). 'I think she's had an accident.'

'Don't worry,' I say, going to the sink to wash sugar and cream from my hands. 'We can sort this out.'

Love On Sunday

They always made love on Sunday mornings. It was a benediction they bestowed on each other – a way of warding off demons.

Tea for Mr Dead

Into the Valley of Death rode the tea trolley. Patients to the right of her, patients to the left, she crashes through the swing doors waking sleepers with a victorious rattle of crockery. Half her cups are gone, three colleagues have fallen to commode duty but she's here, she's got the tea trolley through. Only ten minutes behind time, smack in the middle of visiting hour. It's all right, men. Lie easy. Tea's on its way.

She sweeps the long ward with her nurse's eye. Visitors clutter the view but still she can approximate the correct number of bodies to the right beds, most of them sitting up ready for tea with their tables pulled across in front of them, no one running round naked, dragging expensive equipment by a tube.

She smiles round the ward briefly at no one in particular and pours tea. The brew is thick and mature. Half an hour ago it was weak and without character; now it's strong enough to climb out of the pot unaided. More smiles as she hands it out and prays that no one complains: no time to go back and wait for another kettle to boil, for tea to brew for the right amount of time, to give everyone their cup at once, balance a urinal on your head, change a drip with your teeth, juggle gall-stones with your feet. Stop moaning, everyone in this room is worse off than you.

Her shoes pinch: her sensible nurse's shoes that go *sqwuk* (not on the carpet of the shoe shop when you try them out, but treacherously on contact with a hospital floor). Soft soles don't clatter. A tap-dancing nurse would be unpopular on night duty, but a squeaking nurse, at any time of day, is worse.

Most patients are different when the visitors are there: more friendly, or less so; showing off 'their' nurses or ignoring them.

But the little man is always the same. He asks for nothing, he wants nothing, not even to be asked if he wants something. He's sitting up in bed, his face turned away from her to the space where his visitors have been. As still as a toy no one's playing with.

The air inside her turns to glass.

She should go to him. But first she pours his tea (plenty of milk, one sugar). Another patient is looking. She presses her lips together, but it's not exactly a smile. You can't smile now, she thinks. Draw the curtains round and step inside. Wait. Perhaps if you stay still the little man will lift his head and look. His skin is yellow, like the fat on a side of beef. The lower jaw recedes and drops. If he weren't dead, you'd say he was smiling. His pupils are huge as if he's looking at his greatest love or staring into the dark.

She puts the tea cup down on the bedside cabinet. He looks like one of Peter Pan's lost boys in those pyjamas. He styles his hair like Stanley Matthews. The pillows support him well. He hasn't slipped sideways an inch.

He hadn't wanted to get out of bed that day. 'Just for a minute,' she'd said. 'Sit in the chair while we make up the bed.' He hadn't wanted to be bothered with a wash. 'It will make you feel better,' she'd said. It was the first time she'd ever known him be unwilling. But he was too tired to fight.

His hands are cold but that's no change. His hands were always cold and white as if the blood was needed elsewhere. She puts her fingers on his wrist and then his neck.

Press the bell and wait for someone to come. His tea cools slowly in its cup. In a short while, she will wash him again; she wants to be the one to do it, to roll him over, as gently as if he is still living.

Microclimate

It never rains in my home village. All the weather is caught on the mountains. Rivers flow down into our valley to water the soil and keep the land green. People don't save for a rainy day, but a cloudy one. We have proverbs like: the sun never shines but it boils.

Our school outings take us to rainy places, much as other children are treated to snow. But, since the only things to fall out of our home sky are bird-shit and dead pigeons, the children often cry when they feel the first splatters on their heads. We take them under our mysterious umbrellas beneath which the drumming rain sounds like the feet of vengeful birds.

Safely back inside the coach the children watch droplets wiggle down the windows and look up, wanting to know what invisible hand throws down a river from the sky.

Faith

My invisible friend claims to have lots of invisible chums of her own. I don't believe in them; she says that's just what they say about me.

Frog face

The Princess picked up a frog and kissed it. It turned into a handsome Princess.

The new Princess started kissing other frogs.

'Are you looking for a Prince, too?' said the first Princess, ready to be jealous.

'No,' said the new Princess. 'I like girls. But you *ug*-ly.'

Driving Cinderella

Cinderella's coachman (the ex-rat) couldn't find the way to the ball. For the first time in his life he was able to look a policeman in the eye and suddenly, as if by magic, he was supposed to know how to drive *and* navigate. He couldn't even read the map. The ex-mice seemed to be enjoying themselves though, even if they weren't much good at running in harness.

The ride was so bumpy Cinderella's hair fell down. 'Careful,' she shouted, sticking her head out the window. A branch snagged and tore out her locks by the roots. Cinderella screamed. The mice ran faster, to the top of the wrong mountain.

The magic ended at midnight with Cinderella trapped inside the pumpkin. The mice wanted to eat her free but the ex-coachman said no. He really was a rat.

He gave the pumpkin a kick to set it rolling…

Invisible Friend

My invisible friend isn't speaking to me. We had a terrible row and then she just stopped talking. At first I could tell she was still there because I could hear her tutting. A couple of times she tripped me up and I'm sure once she tried to shove me under a bus. But now I can't hear her at all, so I don't know if she's gone quiet or gone altogether. I don't know whether to save a place for her at table, on the train, or in the pub. When I'm not sure if she's even there, how can I say, 'Sorry, that seat's taken. I'm saving it for an invisible friend.'

But I suppose if I'd done that in the first place she might still be speaking to me now.

The Butcher's Wife

When Matteo saw the butcher's wife bringing beef sausages he leaped backwards and on leaping discovered he could fly.

'I asked for pork,' he shouted. This was true, but not relevant. It was not the beef but the butcher's wife that had startled him into the air. Yet she did not look the kind of woman who could make a man's heart soar, let alone his whole body.

'Come down at once,' she called. 'In a moment you will fall and try to save yourself by holding on to the light fitting for which you are too heavy. There will be plaster in the meat again.' She had begged her husband to buy a strong chain from which such men could swing.

The butcher shrugged. He himself was no longer able to leave the ground and so preferred not to see what was going on right over his head.

Bluebeard's Lament

My fourth wife won't disobey me. I forbid her to take the Bloody Key and unlock the door to the Bloody Chamber and like the three wives before her she says, 'Yes, dear.' Only she seems to mean it. She goes about the house humming; she walks in the garden smiling. It's as if she has a secret of her own. She says, 'Of course you must have your own interests.' I'm so longing to cut off her head.

I thought her compliance was show. Like the others she'd get curious (I was sure). But I've come home unexpectedly now one-hundred-and-twenty-seven times to find her still sitting in the same place, smiling as if she's pleased to see me. I'm beginning to feel like a fool. She gives me such a knowing look each time I kiss her good-bye!

Last week I thought I had her. Her chair was empty and she didn't answer my call. But just as I was running up the stairs to catch her out she came up from the cellar with two bottles of my best wine and asked if I'd be joining her for lunch.

So now I just stay home, spending hour after boring hour alone among the pickled parts of my last three wives, while she reigns, undisputed mistress of the rest of my estate. How I miss my jealous ones: my Molly, my Sally, my Jane. At least they were obliging; at least they took an interest.

Hansel and Gretel

'Where've you kids been?' said their father. 'We were worried sick.'

Hansel and Gretel held hands and looked at the three people on the sofa.

'This lady's a social worker,' said their step-mother, glaring. 'And we're very cross you both forgot to take your mobiles.'

But everyone, except the social worker, knew they didn't have any talk-time left.

'Where have you been?' said the social worker in a friendly voice. 'Would you prefer to speak to me alone?'

'We've been helping an old lady with her oven,' said Gretel.

'Yes,' said Hansel.

They put their hands over their mouths and sniggered.

Once the truth came out (the old lady's sugar supplier found her, half-baked), Hansel and Gretel were separated and sent away. Their story was so unlikely: it just didn't seem possible that an old lady would want to eat children. Not when she had all that gingerbread.

Smile

I'm smiling but can't tell you why. How can I say, 'My invisible friend just made a hilarious comment about your trousers'? Some things you just don't share.

The Longest Date

Our first date. He brought roses, one of which pricked my thumb. A drop of blood welled out. 'Now I suppose I'll have to fall asleep for a hundred years,' I cried. He seized my thumb and sucked it clean. Then he told me all about himself: his taste in films, clothes, footwear, books, beer, holiday destinations, food, funfair rides…At some point I dozed off.

A hundred years later I wake up. Next to me are two piles of dust: one large, one small. Analysis shows the large one to be the remains of his body and the small one the remains of some paper. I imagine he wanted to leave me a record of everything he had to say, including: 'Today, I sat all day by your side. Again, I tried the kiss – nothing.'

I wipe my lips, sigh over the big pile of dust – and blow him away.

Rapunzel Don't Bob Your Hair

The phone rang in Rapunzel's room. It was Princey.

'Are you working?' he said. 'Or can I tempt you to dinner and a night of uncompromising sex?' He was longing to feel the weight of her hair.

'Sounds good,' said Rapunzel. 'But I'm stuck on the top floor. The workmen have gone off and left me without a staircase.'

'Ah,' said Princey. He was all for Rapunzel upgrading her property, he just didn't want to get too involved in case it meant wearing unflattering overalls.

'If only I hadn't had my hair bobbed, you could have climbed up to see me,' said Rapunzel.

Princey said nothing.

'Ironic isn't it?' Rapunzel went on. 'After all those years of trailing that plait around…'

Princey was silent.

'You could always bring a ladder,' said Rapunzel.